Limerick County Library

30012 00523105 4

LEABHARLANN

C LUIMNI

MARIE-LOUISE FITZPATRICK is an award LIF author-illustrator,

whose books *Izzy and Skunk* and *You, Me and the Big Blue Sea*

have both won the Bisto Book of the Year award.

Her warm and distinctive style has attracted fans from all over the world.

Beth, the heroine of *Silly Mummy, Silly Daddy*, is based on

Marie-Louise's own niece. You can read more about Beth's adventures

in Marie-Louise's second book for Frances Lincoln, *Silly School*.

WITHDRAWN FROM STOCK

KU-190-233

WITHDRAWN FROM STOCK

005231.05.
LIMERICK
COUNTY LIBRARY

For Beth, at last! – *M-L.F.*

Silly Mummy, Silly Daddy copyright © Frances Lincoln Limited 2006
Text and illustrations copyright © Marie-Louise Fitzpatrick 2006

The right of Marie-Louise Fitzpatrick to be identified as the author and illustrator
of this work has been asserted by her in accordance with the
Copyright, Designs and Patents Act, 1988 (United Kingdom).

First published in Great Britain in 2006 by
Frances Lincoln Children's Books, 4 Torriano Mews,
Torriano Avenue, London NW5 2RZ
www.franceslincoln.com

First paperback edition 2007

All rights reserved

No part of this publication may be reproduced, stored in a retrieval
system, or transmitted, in any form, or by any means, electrical,
mechanical, photocopying, recording or otherwise without
the prior written permission of the publisher or a licence
permitting restricted copying. In the United Kingdom
such licences are issued by the Copyright Licensing Agency,
Saffron House, 6-10 Kirby Street, London EC1N 8TS.

British Library Cataloguing in Publication Data
available on request

ISBN 978-1-84507-592-7

Printed in Singapore

1 3 5 7 9 8 6 4 2

Silly Mummy, Silly Daddy

Marie-Louise Fitzpatrick

F

FRANCES LINCOLN
CHILDREN'S BOOKS

Beth won't smile today.

Silly Mummy.

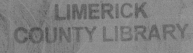

Clip-clop, clip-clop, clip-clop, clip-clop.

Silly Daddy.

LIMERICK COUNTY LIBRARY

Silly Granny.

Silly Grandad.

COB23105
LIMERICK
COUNTY LIBRARY

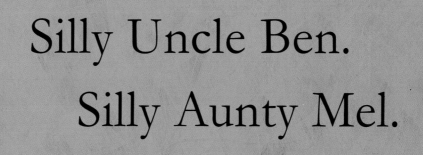

Silly Uncle Ben.
Silly Aunty Mel.

LIMERICK
COUNTY LIBRARY

Sillybillies.

Here comes Ann.

Clever big sister!

LIMERICK
COUNTY LIBRARY

MORE STORIES FROM
FRANCES LINCOLN CHILDREN'S BOOKS

SILLY SCHOOL
Marie-Louise Fitzpatrick
Beth doesn't want to go to silly school!
She doesn't want to go for storytime, or painting, or singing.
Will anyone be able to change her mind?

ISBN 978-1-84507-469-2

I HAVE FEELINGS
Jana Novotny Hunter
Illustrated by Sue Porter
Everybody has feelings – especially me and you!
Waking up is my best time – then I'm feeling happy.
And when we go to the park I feel really excited.
But when my baby sister gets first turn on the swing, I start feeling jealous!

ISBN 978-0-7112-1734-8

WITHDRAWN FROM STOCK

I CAN DO IT!
Jana Novotny Hunter
Illustrated by Lucy Richards
Little Guinea Pig can do all sorts of things!
He can pound his playdough, use his paws to scribble in the sand
and bang his drum when he wants to be LOUD!

ISBN 978-1-84507-127-1

Frances Lincoln titles are available from all good bookshops.
You can also buy books and find out more about your favourite titles,
authors and illustrators on our website: www.franceslincoln.com